Together

Jane Simmons

Alfred A. Knopf · New York

For Cassy, Glenn, Poppy, Pan, and Sheba

Mousse

NUT

THIS IS A BORZOI BOOK PUBLISHED BY ALFRED A. KNOPF

Copyright © 2006 by Jane Simmons

All rights reserved.
Published in the United States by Alfred A. Knopf, an imprint of Random House Children's Books, a division of Random House, Inc., New York.
Originally published in Great Britain in 2006 by Orchard Books. First American edition 2007.

KNOPF, BORZOI BOOKS, and the colophon are registered trademarks of Random House, Inc.

www.randomhouse.com/kids

Educators and librarians, for a variety of teaching tools, visit us at
www.randomhouse.com/teachers

Library of Congress Cataloging-in-Publication Data
Simmons, Jane.
Together / Jane Simmons. — 1st American ed.
p. cm.
SUMMARY: Two dogs, Mousse and Nut, learn that even though they may like different things, they can still be best friends.
ISBN: 978-0-375-84339-6 (trade) — ISBN: 978-0-375-94339-3 (lib. bdg.)
[1. Dogs—Fiction. 2. Best friends—Fiction. 3. Friendship—Fiction.] I. Title.
PZ7.S59182To   2007
[E]—dc22
2006022734

The illustrations in this book were created using acrylic paints.

MANUFACTURED IN MALAYSIA

May 2007   10 9 8 7 6 5 4 3 2 1   First American Edition

When Mousse met Nut, it was raining.

"Hello," said Mousse.

"Hello," said Nut.

They smiled at each other.
The rain stopped and sunshine
broke through the clouds.

"What a wonderful day!"
said Mousse.

"Wonderful!" said Nut.

Every day the sun shone and
every day Mousse sat with Nut . . .

or walked with Nut . . .

or played and giggled with Nut.

"You're my best friend!" said Mousse.
"You're mine!" said Nut.

Everything was wonderful.

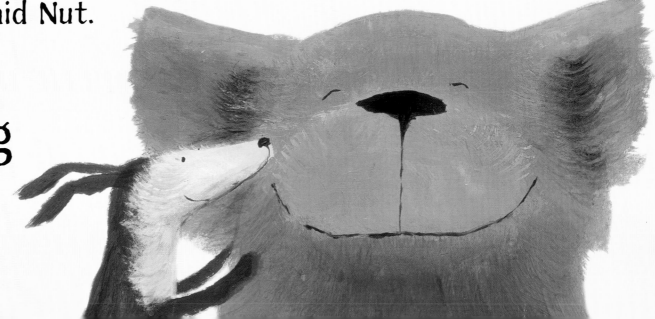

But one day, Nut jumped on top of a wall.
"I can't jump that high," cried Mousse. "Come down!"
"No, I like it up here!" said Nut.

Later, Mousse paddled in the water.
"I can't swim," frowned Nut. "Come out!"

"No, I love it in here!" said Mousse.

Soon, they couldn't agree on anything.

"It's too hot
in the sun."

"It's too cold in
the shade."

"You're too fast."

"You're too slow."

Mousse's best bone was . . .
too **big!**

Nut's favorite biscuit was . . .
too tiny!

"Let's play in my house,"
tried Mousse.

"It's horrible, muddy, and cold," moaned Nut. "I like it this way," said Mousse.

"Let's play at my house," said Nut.

But it was too small.

Dark clouds gathered outside.
"You're not my best
friend anymore,"
said Mousse unhappily.
"You're not mine,
then," said Nut.

Everything
was horrible.

"Goodbye," said Mousse.

"Goodbye," said Nut.

It started to rain.

Mousse swam alone . . .

walked alone . . .

and chewed
her bone alone.

Nut sat in the rain alone.

They both went home alone . . .

and missed each other more than ever.

It was still raining when
Mousse went to find Nut.

"I want to be friends
again," said Mousse.
"Me too!" said Nut.

They smiled at each other.
The rain stopped and sunshine
broke through the clouds.

"What a wonderful day!"
said Mousse.

"Wonderful!" said Nut.

From then on, every day,
Mousse and Nut sat together . . .

and played and giggled together.

Even though they did
different things . . .

they did them **together**.

Whether it was sunshine or rain . . .

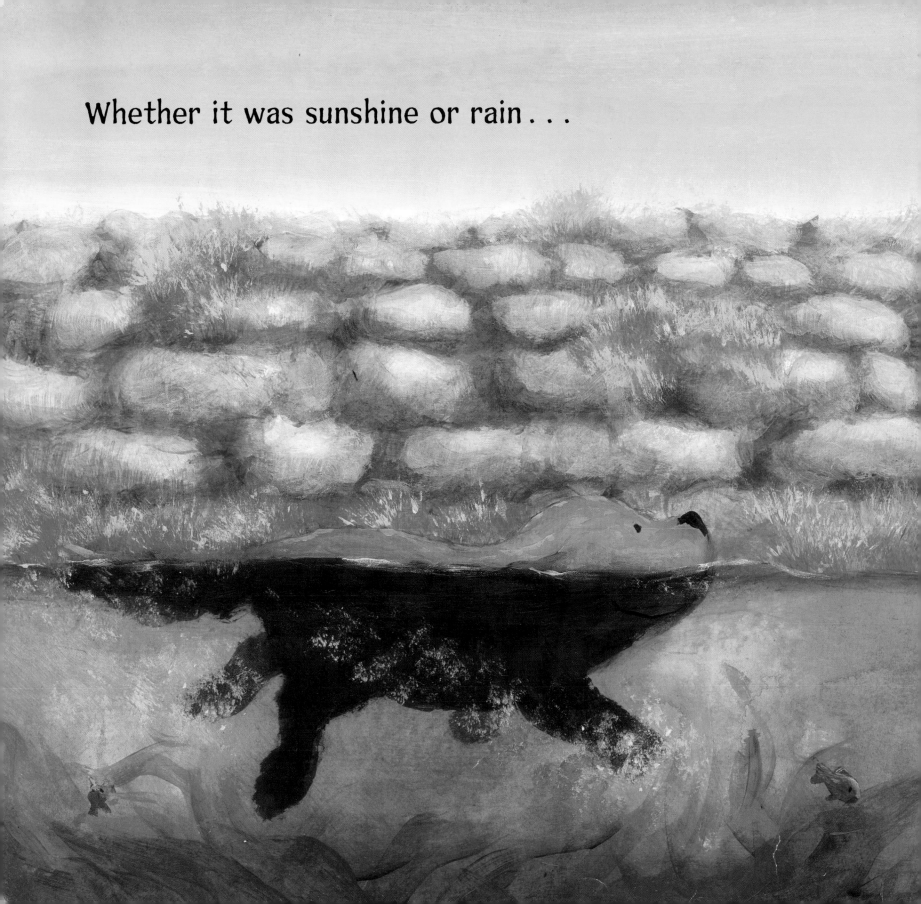

every day was wonderful . . .

. . . and so was every night.